# Sweet Hearts for
# Dolly

### A Bugleberry Book ™

*Written by Ruth Brook*
*Illustrated by Vala Kondo*

## Troll Associates

*Library of Congress Cataloging in Publication Data*

Brook, Ruth.
   Sweet hearts for Dolly.

   Summary: Dolly's friends persuade her to play with
her mother's new hat, with disastrous results, but then
they share the blame when she gets in trouble.
   [1. Hats—Fiction.  2. Conduct of life—Fiction]
I. Kondo, Vala, ill.  II. Title.
PZ7.B78964Sw    1988    [E]    86-30732
ISBN 0-8167-0906-8 (lib. bdg.)
ISBN 0-8167-0907-6 (pbk.)

One cloudy morning, the Bugleberries were sitting on Dolly's front porch, trying to decide what game to play.

"Let's play house," said Dolly. "I'll be the mother. Skip will be the father. Lolly will be the baby. Bo and Betty will be the grandpa and grandma. And, everyone else will be aunts and cousins."

They all agreed.

Just then, Mr. Pipe, the mailman, came up the porch steps. He was delivering a big box.

"Good morning, Dolly!" he called. "I have a package for your mother. Please be sure to give it to her."

Dolly took the package and carried it into her parents' bedroom. All the Bugleberries followed her.

"What's in the box?" asked Toony.

"I'm not sure," said Dolly, "but I think it must be my mother's new hat."

"Oooh," sighed Rosie. "It must be beautiful."

"Let's open the box and see," said Bo.

"I don't think I should," Dolly said. "It's for my mother."

"We'll only take a tiny little peek," said Toony.

"There's nothing wrong with that," added Jingle.

"Well, maybe you're right," Dolly said.
She started to unwrap the package.
Then she stopped.
"I'll open the box for you," said Skip.
"Yes," said Bo. "Open the box."
Dolly had a funny feeling in her stomach,
but she did not want to disappoint her
friends. "Well, all right," she said. "But
please be very careful."

Skip opened the box, and they all looked inside. There was a big beautiful hat with pink flowers and shiny ribbons on it.

Betty took the hat out of the box and put it on Dolly's head.

"Oooooohhh," said everyone. "You look so pretty—just like your mother."

Dolly looked in the mirror. She felt all grown-up and beautiful.

"You should wear that hat while we play house," said Betty. "After all, you *are* the mother."

"Yes," everybody said. "You must wear the hat."

Dolly agreed to wear the hat for just a little while. She said she would put the hat back before her mother came home.

Then everybody went to Dolly's room to dress up.

Skip cut out a paper mustache and pasted it under his nose.

Toony found a string of beads in the toy chest and put them around her neck.

Betty used some cotton and tissue paper to make a wig, and Rosie put a tablecloth around her shoulders for a shawl.

Now Lolly had to be dressed up to look
like a baby.

Skip held Lolly while Dolly dressed her in
a doll's dress. Then Dolly put a bonnet on
Lolly's head and tied it under her chin.
Finally, she fitted little booties on Lolly's
hind paws.

Everyone thought Baby Lolly looked cute.
But Lolly did not look happy.

Skip put Baby Lolly into the doll carriage and wheeled her out onto the porch.

Lolly started to bark.

"Hush, baby," said Dolly. "I'll carry you in my arms."

But when Dolly bent down to pick up her baby, her mother's new hat fell right on top of Lolly's head.

Lolly jumped out of the carriage and ran down the porch steps and into the street.

All the Bugleberries chased after Lolly.
But she was too fast for them. She ran to
the end of Horn Lane, around the corner to
Half Note Road, up Bugle Boulevard, past
McBugle's Bugleburger, all the way to
Piccolo Park. She ran into the park, past
the statue of Clara Nett, and down to
Woodwind Lake.

Before they could stop her, Lolly ran
straight toward the edge of the water.
     *Splash!* Into the lake went Baby Lolly—
hat and all.
     "Oh, no!" cried Dolly. "My mother's hat!
It's ruined!"

Skip fished the wet hat out of the lake.

Dolly could not stop crying. "What shall I tell my mother? She'll be so angry! I just know it!" she sobbed.

"Maybe the hat will dry, and your mother won't mind," said Jingle.

"Maybe you can hide the hat," suggested Bo.

"Maybe you should say you don't know who ruined the hat," said Betty.

Everyone had a different suggestion, but Dolly knew that she would have to tell her mother the truth.

Dolly took the wet hat and ran home.
Lolly followed after her.
   "Where is Dolly going?" asked Toony.
   "Dolly is going home," Skip explained.
"She has to tell her mother about the hat."
   They all stared as Dolly ran away.

The next morning the Bugleberries came to call for Dolly. But Dolly could not come out to play. She had a lot of extra chores to do.

While her mother went downtown to get a new hat, Dolly had to dry the dishes, dust her bookshelves, put her toys away, pull dandelions out of the lawn, give Lolly a bath, and set the table.

"I don't think I'll ever get finished," Dolly sighed.

DRY DISHES
DUST BOOKS
PUT AWAY TO
PULL WEEDS
LOLLY'S BATH
ASH
S
TH

"Why can't Dolly play with us?" asked Toony.

"She's being punished for taking her mother's hat," said Skip.

"But it wasn't Dolly who took the hat out of the box," said Toony. "It was Betty. I saw her."

"That's true," said Betty. "But Skip is the one who opened the box."

"Bo asked me to open it," said Skip.

"That's right," said Bo. "But Jingle told Dolly to wear the hat."

"But Lolly is the one who ran into the water with the hat," said Jingle.

"I guess we're all to blame," Rosie said.

Later that day, Dolly heard her mother's car pull into the driveway. Then she heard a lot of voices.

Dolly looked out of the window and saw all the Bugleberries. They were carrying mops and pails and sponges.

The Bugleberries explained to Dolly's mother that they were *all* to blame for taking the hat. They asked Dolly's mother to forgive them. Now they wanted to help Dolly with her chores.

Dolly heard what her friends were saying. Then she saw a big smile on her mother's face.

"Bugleberries to the rescue!" they shouted as they marched into Dolly's house. "How can we help you, Dolly?"

Dolly showed them her list of chores.

They all got right down to work. Skip dusted the bookshelves. Toony, Bo, and Baby pulled dandelions out of the lawn. Betty and Jingle gave Lolly a bath. Rosie set the table, and Dolly finished putting all her toys into her toy chest.

Before long, they were finished with all the work that had to be done. It was time to go home.

Dolly thanked her friends and walked to the door with them. Just then, they saw eight little boxes standing beside the big hat box. Each box had a name written on it.

Betty, Bo, Baby, Toony, Rosie, Jingle, and Skip opened their packages.

A big heart-shaped cookie was inside each box with a note that said:

A SWEET HEART
FOR
A SWEETHEART!

"I guess your mother has forgiven us," said Betty.

Dolly looked at her mother's hat box, but she did not open it. Instead, she opened the little box that had her name on it.

She looked inside the box and smiled.

There were two sweet hearts for Dolly.